He spent his days sniffing flowers, snoozing in leafy glades, snacking on berries and generally taking it nice and easy.

But sometimes in the evenings he would climb up to the top of the cliff and watch the twinkling lights down in the valley below. He wondered what they were, and what went on there. Perhaps he would go there tomorrow, or sometime next week...

One day whilst he was reclining
in his favourite spot a
strange little bug flew up
and hit him on the nOse.

It spoke very quickly in a squeaky voice and kept gasping for breath, but eventually Bartholomew managed to work out what it was saying.

It seemed obvious the little creature couldn't do this alone and being a kindly bear, with nothing much in particular planned for the day, **Bartholomew** agreed to help him in his quest.

They didn't have a second to lose.

QUICK! BUZZ

Cradling the small insect

in his big paws

Bartholomew clambered his way

to the

bottom

of

the

cliff.

A frog directed them through the stinking swamps.

And over the w a t e r f a l l s

Until eventually they arrived at a huge concrete road.

Bartholomew was devastated.

He couldn't read that well but he knew that 117 was a very big number, and so 117 miles must be a very long way, and that a very long way was sure to take much more than a day to walk. They'd never make it in time.

He sat down by the edge of the road with the bug in the palm of his paw. He didn't know how he would tell him the bad news.

Just then a huge truck pulled up and a
hairy-faced man got out, stood beside
the road and began to whistle.

Bartholomew and the bug very quietly tiptoed
out from the undergrowth, climbed on to the back
of the truck and hid behind some big boxes.

Neither Bartholomew nor the bug had ever travelled **SO** fast in their lives.

They were there in record-breaking time.
The truck screeched to a halt and Bartholomew
and the bug hopped down to take their first
glimpse of the bright lights of the big city.

But it wasn't what they were expecting at all.
There weren't any bright lights, only tall
grey buildings.

They must have got it wrong somehow.
There weren't any lights anywhere.

The bug tried to hide his disappointment.

But as they wandered through the streets and alleys they began to notice a few twinkling lights appearing: first one, then two, then more and more.

Until the whole place was awash with luminescent glow.
And with the lights came the buzz of thousands of insects of every shape and size, all here for the same reason: TO PARTY!

They rode ↑UP & DOWN↓ in ELEVATORS.

They drove about in LIMOUSINES.

They dressed up in Fancy clothes.

They sang.

They danced till Bartholomew thought his legs would drop off-

and some of the bug's did!

And just as Bartholomew thought he could dance no more and the first whispers of dawn began to peep their way over the horizon, he noticed the bug staring into the eyes of a rather pretty lady-bug, and he thought it was probably time for him to go home.

Bartholomew bade farewell to his
insect friends and thanked
them for such a wonderful day.

Until with a FRIZZLE-FRAZZLE
sound they were gone altogether.

COOL! CRAZEEE! THANK YOU MR BEAR!

Bartholomew never went back to the bright lights of the big city.

But at the end of each day, when he sits and watches them from his mountain top, he always thinks of his little bug friend and the fantastic day they spent there together.

BEAR FACTS GRIZZLY BEARS

ARE FOUND IN WESTERN NORTH AMERICA, MAINLY IN MOUNTAINOUS REGIONS. THEY SPEND MOST OF THEIR LIVES AS SOLITARY NOMADS MOSEYING AROUND THEIR RANGE, TRAVELLING KNOWN TRAILS, SEEKING KNOWN REPOSITORIES OF FOOD AND FINDING SECLUDED DAY BEDS FOR SNOOZING. GRIZZLY BEARS CAN LIVE FOR UP TO 25 YEARS.

BUG FACTS CRANE-FLIES

ARE VERY COMMON. THEY SPEND MOST OF THEIR LIVES AS LARVAE BENEATH THE GROUND, EVENTUALLY EMERGING AS ADULTS IN LATE SUMMER AND EARLY FALL. THEY DO NOT FEED NOR DO THEY BITE OR STING. THEIR UNGAINLY FLIGHTS ARE THOUGHT TO ACT AS BOTH A SOCIAL ACTIVITY AND AN AWKWARD KIND OF COURTSHIP DISPLAY. THEY ARE ATTRACTED TO LIGHTS AND MAY GET INTO THE HOUSE BY MISTAKE WHERE THEY GENERALLY DIE. CRANE FLY ADULTS ONLY LIVE FOR ONE OR TWO DAYS AT MOST. IN ENGLAND THEY CARRY THE COMMON NAME OF DADDY-LONG-LEGS.

BOOK FACTS

NEAL GOT THE IDEA FOR THIS BOOK WHILST CAMPING IN THE SIERRA NEVADA MOUNTAINS. HE DIDN'T SEE ANY BEARS BUT SAW PLENTY OF BUGS. THIS BOOK IS DEDICATED TO ALL THE LITTLE CREATURES OF THE WORLD.

FRIENDS FOR A DAY BY NEAL LAYTON

British Library Cataloguing in Publication Data. A catalogue record of this book is available from the British Library.

ISBN 978 1 444 92825 9

FSC
www.fsc.org
MIX
Paper from responsible sources
FSC® C104740